BE FLEXIBLE WITH YOUR GOALS

SWATI SHARMA

Copyright © Swati Sharma
All Rights Reserved.

This book has been published with all efforts taken to make the material error-free after the consent of the author. However, the author and the publisher do not assume and hereby disclaim any liability to any party for any loss, damage, or disruption caused by errors or omissions, whether such errors or omissions result from negligence, accident, or any other cause.

While every effort has been made to avoid any mistake or omission, this publication is being sold on the condition and understanding that neither the author nor the publishers or printers would be liable in any manner to any person by reason of any mistake or omission in this publication or for any action taken or omitted to be taken or advice rendered or accepted on the basis of this work. For any defect in printing or binding the publishers will be liable only to replace the defective copy by another copy of this work then available.

This story I dedicate to the girl who struggles during her student life. In this story, I want to represent how one girl struggles outside of the home. And how boys lived outside of the home. Most others girls faced problems in their life. So in this story, I just want to represent women's empowerment, and how she struggles and reaches her peak point. How does one girl balance the professional as well as personal life? In this story, we couldn't say the boys have no struggles they have different kinds of struggles in their lives. So just here I wanted to point out what is the difference between both the struggle and how both are important for society. They both have equal value in society. So, this is a small story that can represent the student life during the time of college and how they stay at the hostel.

Contents

1. Chapter 1 — 1

2. Chapter 2 — 2

3. Chapter 3 — 4

4. Chapter 4 — 5

5. Chapter 5 — 6

6. Chapter 6 — 7

7. Chapter 7 — 8

8. Chapter 8 — 9

9. Chapter 9 — 10

10. Chapter 10 — 11

11. Chapter 11 — 12

12. Chapter 12 — 13

13. Chapter 13 — 14

14. Facts — 15

15. Facts — 16

16. Facts — 17

17. Facts — 18

18. Sharing Stories — 19

Conclusion:- — 21

CHAPTER ONE

After completing my higher school education I had the to courage join the college. Often college students shared their own experiences. How they eat in the canteen, how they enjoy with friends, and how they spend fun time by using mass bunk. And the imagination of college life was wonderful. But I couldn't say only imagination was wonderful, my college and hostel life was also wonderful. Where I met a lot of friends some friends kept in my touch, some are married, and some went abroad for higher study. I met other people also during my college time who teaches me a lot. I learned a lot from my teachers they play role models in my life. They were my teachers but sometimes they helped me as a friend.

So waking up in the early morning and ready to go to college was the unique experience of my life. I and my friends enjoyed the snacks from the canteen, especially we eat the "samosa" rissole. And I always remember the sip of tea from my college canteen. The time was imaging. Now I represent the story of how life teaches when you are a student.

CHAPTER TWO

My grandfather and my father went to the college during admission time, everywhere students are rushing. One lecture is over and the second lecture starts. I wondered to see the atmosphere. My grandfather and my father eat the snacks there. I feel my life was on a different level, I entered heaven. I met their newly admitted students who were my classmates. I could not express my feelings at that time.

My hometown was far away from the college so I also got admission to the hostel. There are three set rooms available and the other's two girls from a different department. Wake up in the early morning and run fast towards the mess for the breakfast. And then going for the lecture, and again coming into the mess for lunch was a different level of enjoyment in my life.

But there was a difference where we get news how boys are going outside for the enjoyment but in girls hostel never permit to go outside after 5 PM.

I always raise this question still in my mind why is society creating this much difference between the boys and girls. Where boys can go anywhere at the night time but we girls never go outside. I know if you are a girl you have this kind of restriction.

Questions?

i. So still girls have no power in society?

v. Why do they all say about women's empowerment?

v. Why girls have had no freedom as boys?

v. Is girls and boys equal in society?

v. Why in some families are people happy during the birth of a boy?

v. Why do all parents not prefer their girls send outside the study.

CHAPTER THREE

Now my first day in the college where I was introduced to my new classmates. We dared to know about everyone. So after the lecture when we get time we asked a lot of questions regarding study, place, etc. Now the next day came and now the band has been starting to create with us. Saturday came and now we make a small plan for the trip, but I had feared how we could our first mask bunk, the scenario was wonderful during the student life. So now we are all friends met in front of the college gate, and start making plans for how we can reach the destination. So we booked one auto and started our first trip full of craziness. On the way rain has been started we enjoyed the rainy day and finally reached the destination.

We all reached the waterpark, and the waterpark's view was "amazing". Where we all booked our tickets and change our dresses.

Now we are ready to enjoy the swimming pool. We start jumping and swimming, and enjoy the full of craziness. We enjoyed the dance party too in the water. And the sun rises to set up, and now it's time to return home. We ate some snacks and started to return at the home. And after reaching the home we started to share the picks. The moment was memorable.

CHAPTER FOUR

With these, all my friends in college time was flowing very frequently and we passed every semester in our graduation. And enjoy every moment very nicely. I always got the first rank and, one day our college organize prize distribution functions for the achievers. So I got a notification from the side of the college, we were excited to get our prizes. It was a great time in my life. After that, we clicked the pictures and went somewhere and enjoy the moment by eating ice cream. After that, I returned to my home, and I received several messages of best wishes, my family was so happy to know about my achievements. It was the most memorable day of my life. Now I want to celebrate my happiness with family and by doing a pizza party.

CHAPTER FIVE

For me it was a great time during my graduation, yes its true achievements are part of my life but the real moments that I spent and enjoy with my friends. In college sometimes we went to see movies, outing and enjoy ourselves a lot there. And some of my friends are now Miss missing. Some love stories also initiate with our higher education. Then during my graduation, I was preparing for the entrance exam

"study" "hard work" "IM VERY HECTIC" but finally I cleared the exam. And have a plan to go new college. Now I'm excited but also nervous about how would I manage in the new place with new friends, but I know God is always with me. Finally, the exam was over, and I was excited to go to a new place.

CHAPTER SIX

I didn't have any idea how my vacations finished very frequently, because every day I started to count the days, shopping and much more work. Finally, I remember the day when I started the journey, I woke up early morning I was happy but sad, I was unable to do eye contact with my mother. Finally, I started the journey when I met my mother she hugged me tightly and start crying. Even I was crying latterly. Finally, my father drop me at the railway station and I sat on the berth, after a few minutes new passengers also came onto the train. And now the train leaving the station, it was a sad and happy moment for me. I was excited to go, but I was sad inside because I was missing my pets(rabbits), and my family. But after some time I was feeling normal, in this journey, my grandfather was with me, so we start gossiping with each other, enjoying the serenity of the places.

The view inside the train was different where I noticed a lot of things, really my India is beautiful and truly expressed in the song " DESH RANGILA RANGILA MERA". Every single mile change the color of the soil, change language, different cultures people, and different food items it was a great experience in my life. Finally, we reached our destination.

CHAPTER SEVEN

Finally, I reached the city of dream, where I plan to start my new career. We booked one homestay, and now I and my grandfather went outside and searched for a portion of food just like in the story "thirsty crow" as he searched for water. Because we are pure vegetarians, especially my grandfather, I'm under the category of vegetarian. But it was really difficult to search for food at "queen of the ocean" finally we saw one shop, and we were happy finally we search for hed something. But it was a great struggle to eat south Indian food when you belong to North India. But we did it. After that we went to see, the sea was "salt in the air, sand in my hair". It was the great miracle of my life. The most important rain at queen of the ocean suddenly started very heavy rain and stop.

CHAPTER EIGHT

The next day I and my grandfather went for the interview, I was excited but very nervous, and a lot of thoughts came into my mind. But finally, I crack the interview, and that day I and my grandfather celebrate the day. We spent 3-to 4 days together, and now I know it's time to join the hostel and for my grandfather to return to his hometown. We both were sad, and finally, I came to the hostel and he returned home by flight. For me difficult to adjust to a new city where I had no friends, I spent 3 days alone at the hostel. Now Monday morning and I was excited to go new college, when I reached college my new teacher welcome me because I was a single girl who came from North India to South India. And after that I met with my new friends, the problem was they were unable to understand my "Punjabi", and I was unable to understand their "Malayalam". With time I started to

adjust me to the new atmosphere. And I also learned some new words, such as video poya, which means where you are going, khat chu which means had your dinner, Marya, which means rain, and learn many more.

CHAPTER NINE

We had a scheduled 9 to 5, and after that completing homework, sometimes I feel tired, hectic, and nervous. But there my friends were very supportive of me, every Sunday we all go for an outing to enjoy snakes, but it doesn't mean I missed my home food, especially mom-made food.

My college organizes an annual function, now I also want to participate, then my friends raise my confidence, they know the language and I can understand only lyrics. I prepared the dance with the help of lyrics, I got a prize and all the people present at the function appreciated me. I was so happy. I and my friends go for outings and enjoy every moment. One day my friend offer me to go to her hometown, then I decided to go there, it was a beautiful destination. I enjoyed the serenity of the hills, and the people love me

a lot. They were christened and with them, I visited the Church. And also visited more beautiful destinations. After spending 4-5 days at their home finally we both returned to the hostel. And again classes started. After one week vacations will be started and had the plan to go home town. I didn't have any idea how I spend one week, I was so excited to go home after a long time.

CHAPTER TEN

At that time in India, there was no online booking system as the system is updated these days. So I and my friends went outside and searched for the air ticket booking. Finally, we saw one shop and I booked my air ticket first time. This is my first journey on the flight. I was alone somewhere I was excited to go home, but at the same time, I was nervous. Oh God, now what will happen to me, if the airplane falls if something happened to me. Because during my childhood I always watched plane crashes on the discovery channel. That thoughts somewhere impact my brain. But as a first impression is the last impression, same as it is first journey excitement is first the second journey never compete for the excitement as the same way.

Finally, the day came, it was Wednesday, I woke up a lot of time, I saw a dream I was late, I missed my plane, but finally, I woke up and

was ready to go, my friends drop me at the airport. They were nice. Finally, I entered the airport. Everything was new for me, I was nervous, and as well as I was excited. But during the time of check-in, I met with the person, and just we start a conversation Hi, Hello, and finally, he taught me a lot about things. Now it's time to be on board the plane, I was like 'wow what a big bus'. Finally, we were ready for the takeoff, and I was feeling like, I'm a bird and fly in the air. It was a great experience.

CHAPTER ELEVEN

Finally, I reached my home and met with my all family members, I was very happy to meet with my pets. And my family treated me like I 'm a celebrity who came to the home. My mother and grandmother cooked different, different food items for me. My father and grandfather bring a lot of gifts for me. My brother was extremely happy to meet me. I had no idea how two weeks passes very frequently, but now it's time to return to college. But this time I was able to eye contact with my mother. Finally, they drop me at the airport, and after a few hours of the journey, I reached the destination. My friends were very excited to meet me, I bought gifts for them, and they were happy to accept my gifts. Honestly, I had no idea how I spent 2 years with my friends and teachers.

CHAPTER TWELVE

Now it's time to farewell, and we were sad during the red carpet eve. Finally, I return home and enjoyed my holidays. And I plan to start my internship and also explore a new city. And now I planned to visit the new city, the city of "Deccan". Again I and my grandfather are ready for the new journey, in my life he plays a very important role, my father, my grandfather, and my close friend. Finally, I reached the destination with my grandfather in the city of "Deccan". Where I am also ready to learn new things, new language, and new food.

CHAPTER THIRTEEN

The next morning I woke full of energy, had breakfast with my grandfather and we made a plan to go to Shirdi, then we came to the room packed the bag, and start a new journey. In the evening we reached the Sai temple and after worship, we enjoyed the food, and plan to return. Early morning we return to the home and still 3-4 days we both enjoy a lot. And finally, my grandfather returned home and I start my new study chapter in the new city.

CHAPTER FOURTEEN

FACTS

During student life, we learn new things that we never learned in the home atmosphere. Where we learned how to get up early morning and should need to finish breakfast before 9 AM. And then reached your institute time without the help of your mother. After that, after completing our class we return to the hostel before lunch, then start studying, after we woke and reached for tea and snacks. Sometimes we all friends go outside shopping in the evening, spent too much time together doing gossip and backbites what had happened in the college, backbites if we don't like a common person in our classroom. And before gate closing we reached the hostel, and if we late requested the warden to enter the hostel. The moment was marvelous.

FACTS

We were all friends excited to go out for a Sunday outing, collect money according to the budget and book a cab, and reached the destination. But if we are 6 friends always missing two friends reason they have boyfriends and finally they find time during the Sunday. And after the evening when we reached the hostel we shared a full day's enjoyment experience. And next day we all know it's time to go to college, "Monday morning."

And now we understand the value of my teachers, when we were students our teachers always said enjoy student life, it will never come back again, that time we thought why they are said like that, but now we realize the value of their existing words.

CHAPTER SIXTEEN

FACTS

Some students fall in love during the student life, it's not bad but first, we should need focus on the carrier then we think about the marriage life. Because if you settle first you have no worries to plan your future. My aunt said me don't be emotional, and always be irrational during the time of student life. And when you take any single step first you should need to think about the family. Because if you spoil your life during student life you will never get back the same way.

CHAPTER SEVENTEEN

FACTS

One of the interesting facts about student life is if you are a brilliant student and topper of the class. Other students always force you to bunk the class and avoid the test. But it was a great headache for you on one side you are the favorite student of your teachers at the same time your friends. It was a big dilemma in my life. But we never forget the friends and teachers with them we collect a lot of memories during the student life.

CHAPTER EIGHTEEN

SHARING STORIES

My grandfather (I love his name Birbal Dogra) always shares a student life story with us and with my grandmother (her cute name is Urmila Dogra). In 1950 he completed his 10th grade, After that his father, my great-grandfather sent him to college for higher study. He started to live with a cousin, but after a few days, he noticed his cousin's family did not properly behave toward him. Then he said lie hold his bag and came to the hostel, and sat at the one corner. And one friend came to meet her and said one bed was vacant in his room. And finally, he started to play with friends. My grandfather shared with me that they do have not to worry about their study. He said he was always exciting to eat food, and they all friends fail during the house test. And after that they all friends collect money to buy one book and bilaterally he started the study. And after completing their study he returns home and works at the farm. After 2 months one of his friends informedhim about the result. He went to see the result with his friend and was unable to see the result. Then both friends decided to find each other results. Finally, his friend informed him you are passed by getting distinctions. He shared the experience he didn't have an idea he will pass the examination, he decided if he will fail in the examination he will never return home because his father beat him, he will go to Mumbai and start a carrier in the film industry. Now he is 80 years old young man, my best friend and I learned a lot from him, he shared 80 years of experience with me as I mentioned in the book, "parents' arguments affect their children mentally growth" and my grandmother was unable to complete her study. Because at the age of 8 she was engaged to my grandfather, and they always shared the story they didn't have any idea about the marriage life. What I reached here I complete my study only because of my grandmother because she played a very important role in my education, she always inspired me to study and shared her story of how she faced difficulties after her marriage life. So first you should need to be qualified, educated and then you should need to think about the marriage life.

Conclusion:-

What we learned during student life greatly impacts our development. Because sometimes we had a very cooperative atmosphere in the institute, sometimes we noticed partiality, some other factors that we observe during the student life. But overall the student life is the best as compared to office life, and marriage life. We learned a lot during student life, so enjoy the student life fullest, plan trips, make friends, and study harder because it was the best part of our life.

www.ingramcontent.com/pod-product-compliance
Lightning Source LLC
Chambersburg PA
CBHW021158130726
47988CB00004B/1671